MW00873391

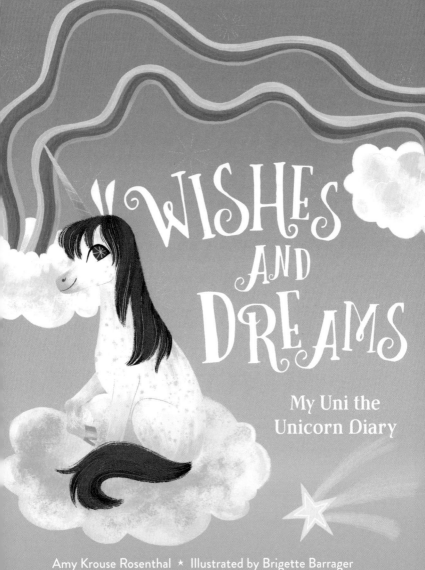

# WISHES AND DREAMS

## My Uni the Unicorn Diary

Amy Krouse Rosenthal ★ Illustrated by Brigette Barrager

POTTER

Have you ever seen a shooting star?
Did you make a wish on it?

.............................................................................

.............................................................................

.............................................................................

.............................................................................

.............................................................................

.............................................................................

.............................................................................

.............................................................................

.............................................................................

.............................................................................

.............................................................................

If you were a unicorn, what would you look like? Draw a picture.

Have you ever seen a rainbow? Have you ever seen a *double* rainbow?

........................................................................

........................................................................

........................................................................

........................................................................

........................................................................

........................................................................

........................................................................

........................................................................

........................................................................

........................................................................

........................................................................

# Do you like rain? Have you ever splashed in a puddle?

.................................................................................................

.................................................................................................

.................................................................................................

.................................................................................................

.................................................................................................

.................................................................................................

.................................................................................................

.................................................................................

.................................................................................

.................................................................................

.................................................................................

.................................................................................

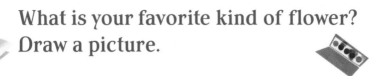

# What is your favorite kind of flower?
# Draw a picture.

**If you could visit the Land of Unicorns, what would you do there?**

.......................................................................................

.......................................................................................

.......................................................................................

.......................................................................................

.......................................................................................

.......................................................................................

.......................................................................................

.......................................................................................

.......................................................................................

.......................................................................................

.......................................................................................

# When was the last time you saw a rainbow?

If you met a forest creature in need, would you help it?

If you could be a unicorn for one day, what would you do? Grant wishes? Run through the meadow? Slide down a rainbow?

........................................................................

........................................................................

........................................................................

........................................................................

........................................................................

........................................................................

........................................................................

........................................................................

........................................................................

List your 5 favorite books.

1.

2.

3.

4.

5.

If you met a unicorn and could wish for anything, what would you wish for?

........................................................................................

........................................................................................

........................................................................................

........................................................................................

........................................................................................

........................................................................................

........................................................................................

........................................................................................

........................................................................................

........................................................................................

Do you have a best friend? What are they like? Draw a picture.

# ⭐ What's your favorite ice cream flavor?

List 5 places you love to go to.

1.

2.

3.

4.

5.

If you could have one superpower, what would it be?

List your top 5 favorite movies.

1.

2.

3.

4.

5.

What's your favorite kind of tree? Draw a picture.

List 3 things you are really good at.

1.

2.

3.

# What's your favorite dessert?

**List 5 ways you can cheer someone up when they feel sad.**

1.

2.

3.

4.

5.

# What is something *you* believe in?

........................................................................................

........................................................................................

........................................................................................

........................................................................................

........................................................................................

........................................................................................

........................................................................................

........................................................................................

........................................................................................

........................................................................................

........................................................................................

**List 3 foods you could eat every day and not get tired of.**

1.

2.

3.

If you could travel anywhere in the whole world, where would you go? Who would you take with you?

..........................................................................................................

..........................................................................................................

..........................................................................................................

..........................................................................................................

..........................................................................................................

..........................................................................................................

..........................................................................................................

..........................................................................................................

..........................................................................................................

..........................................................................................................

## List your 5 favorite colors.

1.
2.
3.
4.
5.

What's your favorite animal? Would you want to have that animal as a pet? What would you name it?

..............................................................................................................

..............................................................................................................

..............................................................................................................

..............................................................................................................

..............................................................................................................

..............................................................................................................

..............................................................................................................

..............................................................................................................

..............................................................................................................

# What is something that you are grateful for?

........................................................................................

........................................................................................

........................................................................................

........................................................................................

........................................................................................

........................................................................................

........................................................................................

........................................................................................

........................................................................................

........................................................................................

Do you have a favorite toy?
Draw a picture of it.

# What's your favorite word?

........................................................................................

........................................................................................

........................................................................................

........................................................................................

........................................................................................

........................................................................................

........................................................................................

........................................................................................

........................................................................................

........................................................................................

........................................................................................

What's the nicest compliment that you've ever received? What's a nice compliment that you can give to someone else?

.................................................................................................................................

.................................................................................................................................

.................................................................................................................................

.................................................................................................................................

.................................................................................................................................

.................................................................................................................................

.................................................................................................................................

.................................................................................................................................

.................................................................................................................................

**What's your favorite thing to do outside?**

..........................................................................................................

..........................................................................................................

..........................................................................................................

..........................................................................................................

..........................................................................................................

..........................................................................................................

..........................................................................................................

..........................................................................................................

..........................................................................................................

..........................................................................................................

..........................................................................................................

List your top 5 favorite things to do just for *fun*.

1.

2.

3.

4.

5.

# List 3 games you love to play.

1.
................................................................

................................................................

................................................................

2.
................................................................

................................................................

................................................................

3.
................................................................

................................................................

................................................................

# What flavor is each color of the rainbow?

**Red is...**

**Orange is...**

**Yellow is...**

**Green is...**

**Blue is...**

**Violet is...**

**Pink is...**

**Who is someone that you are grateful for?**

.......................................................................................................................

.......................................................................................................................

.......................................................................................................................

.......................................................................................................................

.......................................................................................................................

.......................................................................................................................

.......................................................................................................................

.......................................................................................................................

.......................................................................................................................

.......................................................................................................................

.......................................................................................................................

.......................................................................................................................

# List your 5 favorite songs.

1.

2.

3.

4.

5.

# What makes *you* unique?

......................................................................................

......................................................................................

......................................................................................

......................................................................................

......................................................................................

......................................................................................

......................................................................................

......................................................................................

......................................................................................

......................................................................................

......................................................................................

Published in the United States by Clarkson Potter/Publishers, an
imprint of Random House, a division of Penguin Random House
LLC, New York.
clarksonpotter.com

CLARKSON POTTER is a trademark and POTTER with colophon
is a registered trademark of Penguin Random House LLC.

Based on *Uni the Unicorn*, originally published by Random House
Children's Books, a division of Penguin Random House LLC, New
York, in 2014. Copyright © 2014 by Amy Krouse Rosenthal.
Illustrations copyright © 2014 by Brigette Barrager.

ISBN 978-0-593-13712-3

Made in China
05/21

Design by Annalisa Sheldahl

10 9 8 7 6 5 4 3 2 1

First Edition